Winter Dreams

and other such friendly dragons

Joseph J Jukmialis

illustrated by

Barbara A Salvo

To those who dream
And to those who have taught others how.

ISBN 0-89390-010-9
Library of Congress Catalog Card Number
79-64821

Acknowledgements:
Cover design, book design, and all ink wash drawings by Barb Salvo. Though dreams are abstractions of reality sometimes flowing in seas of color, sometimes only black and white pervade the subconscious. As an abstractionist painter who deals primarily with color, her work is often considered dreamlike. To enable one to reach inside and see reality through imagination is one of her greatest pleasures in life. At present she lives and creates in Milwaukee, Wisconsin.

Typography: Maureen Stuart

Published by Resource Publications, Inc., 160 E. Virginia St. #290, San Jose CA, 95112

Printed and bound in the United States of America.   4   3

Contents

Stories Of Winter

Stories Of Dreams

The Season of Winter and the Dreams of our Spirits come into our lives side by side — one from without and one from within. Each is a reflection of the other, and we wonder which is the original.

Winter prepares for birth. She comes as the first of all the seasons. Gifted with anticipation and preparation, she makes ready for new life and sets patterns for the year's colors and shapes. In like manner our Dreams are the planted seeds of what shall be. From our Dreams come forth the shape of our love and the color of our joy.

Winter conceals blessings yet to be discovered. So do dreams. Winter appears draped in gray death hiding the life being shaped. So too do Dreams arrive costumed in all that is unreal — smiling fantasies of hope for still believing children.

Winter is mother and father of all that will be. Without Winter, spring has no life. Without Dreams, the present has no future.

Into our lives wander the Season of Winter and the Dreams of our Spirits. They make their arrival, tugged at by pet dragons who pull and who prod into tomorrow the masters who own them. Thus a Winter which does not give way to spring remains frozen and rigid, and Dreams which are not made flesh cease to be real.

Rejoice then, that you live in the Season of Winter and that you journey among the Dreams of your Spirits. Fear not the friendly dragons that you meet. For you are indeed blessed with a vision for the future and hope for God's people and a spirit that offers life.

Winter Dreams

Sealed
With
A
Dream

Long, long before tomorrow, though it was most certainly since
yesterday, in a village tucked beneath the bountiful covers of a
land simply called Sometime, there lived a potter by the name of
Nicholas. Nicholas and his wife Christina had both been born in
the village and had grown up together in homes whose backyards
and whose families both met. It was no surprise to anyone when
Nicholas and Christina became the village's next Mr. and Mrs.
Together they bought a small plot of land in the middle of the village, and on the land they built their love — with a downstairs

where Nicholas would spin his pottery and an upstairs where Christina would spin a home for the two of them. And while they were never able to have any children of their own, the upstairs and downstairs loves which they built became home for almost everyone in the village. As Nicholas would spin his pottery, passersby would stop and share the day's fortunes — treasures rich and not so rich. And in their upstairs, Christina wove a warm heart from the time given in listening to the tears of a neighbor's pain and drying the troubles of unsettled hearts. In short, the villagers became their children.

What was peculiar, however, about Nicholas' downstairs and Christina's upstairs was the shelves and shelves and shelves of pottery jars, all sealed with dreams and placed on the shelves, never again to be disturbed. No one, it seemed, quite knew the meaning of the task, why there were so many shelves of stopped up pottery jars which never would be sold. While everyone wondered, no one ever asked. They simply wondered. In fact, it was so unusual that even Nicholas would silently ask the question of himself. They were jars of light, that much he knew, but what Nicholas was not sure about was why they were all saved. He simply knew that every day he would go outside and collect two jars of light — one he would seal with a dream and place on a shelf, and the other he would place in his window at night to help anyone who had lost their light. Once, when their love had first begun, Christina had asked him why he saved the jars of light. Nicholas could only say that for as long as he could remember, his own father had done what Nicholas now did day after day. Before he died, he had asked

Nicholas to continue what had been begun even before his father's father's father. Nicholas could not say why it was being done. Nor could he say for how long it had been done. He simply sensed that it needed to be done. What bothered Nicholas most of all was that he and Christina had no child who would continue to save the jars of light after they both would die. That was the one thing about which Nicholas would often worry — silently — yet, nevertheless, worry. And so it was that day after day the number of sealed jars of light grew and grew. The rooms became smaller and smaller as the shelves became more and more numerous. And no one, it seemed, knew why.

One day, as Nicholas spun his pottery, a neighbor stopped by in need of the goodness Nicholas would offer. The neighbor brought with him a heart wearied by the struggles and pains of his family. Nicholas listened, sometimes stopping his work to touch a shoulder, sometimes looking up to touch a heart. After much spun pottery had passed and the neighbor was about to leave, he mentioned to Nicholas how he felt so much darkness. There was so little light in his life, in his heart, in his soul. And then, almost without thinking, Nicholas reached for one of the pottery jars filled with light and sealed long ago. It was dusty; it was old. It came from a time before Nicholas. But it held the gift of light. Nicholas hesitated. Was the light his to give away? Yet, what good was light, he thought, if it could not be poured out into darkness. And so Nicholas held out to the neighbor the jar of light, and he whispered to him, "A gift, a gift of light, for you, if you should ever need a place away from darkness." The neighbor simply smiled — his thank you — in a way which made one wonder if the light in the jar had been set free into the eyes of the one holding it. He left Nicholas to his spinning, and when he returned home to his troubled family he put the jar of light on a shelf above their door. He never opened the jar — he never had need to after that day, for simply knowing that the light was there should he ever need a place away from his darkness was enough light in itself for his troubled family.

That night, after Nicholas had placed a jar of that day's light in his downstairs window, he went upstairs and told Christina of his excitement and joy about the light that he had shared. Christina did not say anything when Nicholas finished his story. There was no need. She knew and Nicholas knew. There was no other need. And with their smiles they touched each other's hearts.

From that day on, whenever anyone in darkness came to Christina's upstairs or Nicholas' downstairs, they would listen to that darkness and heal it with their understanding. Then they would give that person a pottery jar of light sealed with a dream. And to each they would whisper, "A gift, a gift of light, for you, if you should ever need a place away from your darkness."

There were many who came in darkness. Those chained in the darkness of fear or of loneliness. Those finding themselves in the darkness of illness or growing death. There were those who were forgotten or not understood. Those whom no one would forgive. Those in grief and in pain. One by one the jars of light slowly disappeared. So slowly that no one else ever noticed. Each thought they were the only one with the precious gift of light — saved for them if they should ever need a place away from their darkness. And none of those who received a jar ever found a need to open the jar, for simply knowing that it was there was enough light to provide a place away from their darkness.

Many years passed and many jars of light had been shared. The shelves grew empty and yet no one noticed. In the village there was less darkness and more and more light. One night the villagers noticed that there was no light in Nicholas' downstairs window — nor in Christina's upstairs. When morning came the villagers went to the pottery shop. Nicholas was not there. They went upstairs. They called to Nicholas and Christina, but there was no answer. They pushed open the door and found them both — asleep in one another's light — forever. There would be no more jars of light saved for those who needed a place away from darkness. There would be no more spinning, no more upstairs and no more downstairs.

That night all the villagers gathered together to pray by the two long wooden boxes which contained the only real light the village had ever known. After some time had passed, someone arose and walked to the front. On the ground, between the two boxes, the villager placed a pottery jar sealed with a dream. He broke the seal, and lifted out the dream, and then went back to his place. Then another villager came forward, and another, and another, and another. Each person in the village came and placed a pottery jar between the two long wooden boxes. Each broke the seal and lifted out the dream. Each had been in darkness but had been given some light if they should have ever needed a place away from their darkness.

14

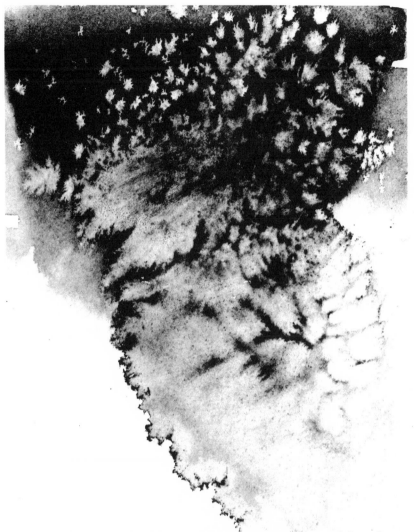

The light from those jars broke into the darkness of that dreary night. It raced to the heavens, and it shattered the gloom. And the light from those thousands of jars joined together in the hollow darkness of that night. And the people looked up in disbelief, and they cried out, "Look! Look, a star!" It was brighter than any star any of them had ever seen — so bright that it overcame the darkness of that night. The people looked at their star, and at one another, and at the dream each one held in his hand, and they knew then that on that night love had been born in their midst.

God was indeed among his people.

A
Sand
Dollar
For
A
Dream

In the after-told stories of everyone else, we were going on a nine day camping trip to the beaches of Florida. We were, it was retold, in search of sun. I alone was aware of another dream aborning in my spirit — it was a dream in search of a sand dollar. Once one gives birth to a dream, be it fulfilled or ever hazy and unclear, one's life is no longer the same. Dreams do that to people, and thus it is that dreaming can be a very dangerous pastime.

Sand dollars, to those who are non-beach dreamers (if such there be), are somewhat similar in appearance to clam shells. They are round, usually two or three inches in diameter, and have on their faces a five pointed star — legend says for the Star of Bethlehem, and five slots — telling of the five wounds of Christ, according to the same legend. They are rarely found on the shore primarily because they are so fragile and are often broken up by the time the tide shifts them upon the beach. I came to the beaches of Florida in dream of a sand dollar.

The beaches were filled with shells — many of them — though most had been beaten by the surf, and what remained was the crushed carcass of the living sea. I walked the beaches hour upon hour, hope upon hope, my eyes scanning the sea's relics like the wandering beacons of prison towers. In time I found pieces of the dream, but they were small — too fractured to be remembered. I had patrolled the beaches in both directions, and I was beginning the process of learning how to live with unborn dreams.

It was then that I learned a lesson from the sea and from the unfound sand dollar. Both, I realized, were much wiser than I, and I knew then why it was that I so often came to the sea. Its wisdom was shared if one listened to the waves. I learned from the sea, that day, that it was better not to find the dreamed of sand dollar for which I lusted. For, you see, once a dream comes true, it is no longer a dream, and its fulfillment carries with it a bit of sadness, for the unfolded mystery is understood and the impossible is made possible. I realized then that I did not wish to find the sand dollar for it gave me a reason to return one day. It kept my spirit alive. I now know that all was not in my control. It was good to desire and not receive, for spirits die when dreams end and creation is choked when all that breathes is the present and the past. I smiled to myself as I realized the sea's true gift — a dream allowed to live. Yet the sea and the sand dollar had not yet completed their lesson.

As I walked home along the sea's sandy rim, I looked down into her shallows, and there I saw a sand dollar. Was it a blessing or a curse? A comedy or a tragedy? Had the sea taught me a lesson — only to destroy the joy I received in learning the lesson? Had she taught me how to dream, only then to shatter that dream, more fragile than the sand dollar itself?

I fearfully lifted the sea's gift — very much aware that in place of the once imagined delight, there now was a weary sadness, for a dream had died. I considered, briefly, the possibility of crushing the treasure, hoping thereby to rebirth the dream. But I quickly realized that dreams live only once. The moment of Camelot had passed.

As I walked on, for some mysterious reason I found other sand dollars. Some I gave away to fellow seekers — though I wondered if it were fair to destroy so easily their dreams. (Being a destroyer of dreams is no pleasant admission, I assure you.) There was a bit of joy in announcing my discovery upon my return, and others shared in my muted delight. In the days that followed more sand dollars were discovered, though I sensed it would have been a greater gift to have been given another dream.

I am home now in wintered Wisconsin, and the souvenir sand dollars lie in state upon my book shelf. While within them there is a hint of joyous sun-beached memories, they also cry out as hollow-shelled reminders of dreams once held.

Of Florida and her days I shall remember many things — good friends shared in peaceful joy, misty nights and warming days, as well as the luxury of lazy time. But of it all I shall not forget the dream she taught me to cherish and then stole before I could even delight in her generosity.

Kingdoms
Queendoms
And
Ourdoms

On the edge of a misty Autumn day, crouched in the would-be shadow of a lonely mushroom, I came upon a dream. He was the last remaining dream of his land for all the others had been long forgotten. As a result they all had died, for dreams can only live if they are remembered. There, enthroned on the stumped remains of a once wise oak, that dream shared with me this story.

There was once a time in the wish-marked hill country of his homeland when there lived a king named Darien. One day one of the king's people, one named Pergoff, came and said to Darien, "My king, I think that I should like to sit upon your throne and be king myself." Darien sat back and, being the wise man that he was, said to himself, "If I say 'no' to this person, the kingdom will be divided for there will be those who will side with me and there will be those who will side with him." And so Darien turned to Pergoff and agreed. "You may be king but only under one condition — that you be king for one year and one day only. And if after one year and one day you yet wish to remain as king, it shall be yours as you request. But should you choose to end your reign as king, then the kingdom shall once again be mine." To Pergoff it seemed quite fair. And thus it was that he agreed to the terms of this most unusual agreement.

On the next day, the first day of his reign, Pergoff gathered all of his people together and announced, "My people, I have called you here to tell you that I am your king." There was only silence, and so he thought they must not have understood him. Again he said, "My people, I have gathered you here to tell you that I am your king." Slowly, one by one, the people turned around and walked away. And Pergoff stood there, a king without a kingdom.

Weeks passed. And Pergoff said to himself, "I know what I will do. I will gather myself an army." And so he sent out word that he was establishing an army, for all kings wage war. Yet when he called for the gathering of his army — no one came. And again Pergoff stood there, a king without a kingdom.

To himself he mused, "No matter. I will be a king who does not wage war. I will legislate laws." And so he wrote out his laws — laws for when people should work and when they should not work, laws for when they should gather food and when they should distribute food, laws for when they should go out and laws for when they should stay home. But no one followed Pergoff's laws. No matter what he legislated, people continued to do what they wished. And there Pergoff stood, without an army, without the power to legislate, a king without a kingdom.

Weeks passed. And months passed. And soon it was drawing near the end of one year and one day. And Pergoff said, "One final thing I will do before I end my reign as king. I will levy a tax." And Pergoff taxed all his people, for he wanted to be a wealthy king. But no one paid their taxes.

In the end, Pergoff stood before Darien without an army, without laws, a poor king without a kingdom, and he said to Darien, "A year and a day have passed. I do not wish to be king any longer. You may be king again. But tell me — why did I fail?" Darien looked at Pergoff and sadly but wisely explained. "You failed because real kings do not wage war, they wage peace. You failed, Pergoff, because real kings do not legislate laws, they legislate love. You failed because real kings amass only a wealth of wisdom and no more. For you see, Pergoff," said Darien, "the only kingdom that makes any difference is the kingdom within each of us. And that is what we are called to rule."

Pergoff then asked Darien, "But why is it that you can be king, king over all these people, and I cannot?" "The difference," said Darien, "is that my reign will last only until each person's kingdom within him is made known. It will last only as long as I can call every man and every woman, every boy and every girl, to be king or queen, prince or princess of the kingdom which lies deep within their spirit. Once all people have discovered *that* kingdom, then *my* reign will end. No longer will there be any need to be king; no longer will there be any need to rule for we will live in peace and in love and have all wisdom. We shall be the kingdom."

Thus the story ended; and the dream who had shared it looked pleased for, you see, it is only when dreams are shared that life is truly given. And when life is given, when we do live in peace and in love, then we will have the wisdom to know that Christ is King — for you see, we are the Christ.

Once
Upon
A
Dream

It seems we never remember when a dream begins, or when it is born, or when it takes its first breath. For whatever the reason, its genesis quickly loses shape. Almost instantly we are spiraled into the vortex of an unfolding dream — captivated, enchanted, hypnotized. What follows here is the story of such a dream. Whether or not it reflects the truth of reality, each of us must answer for ourselves.

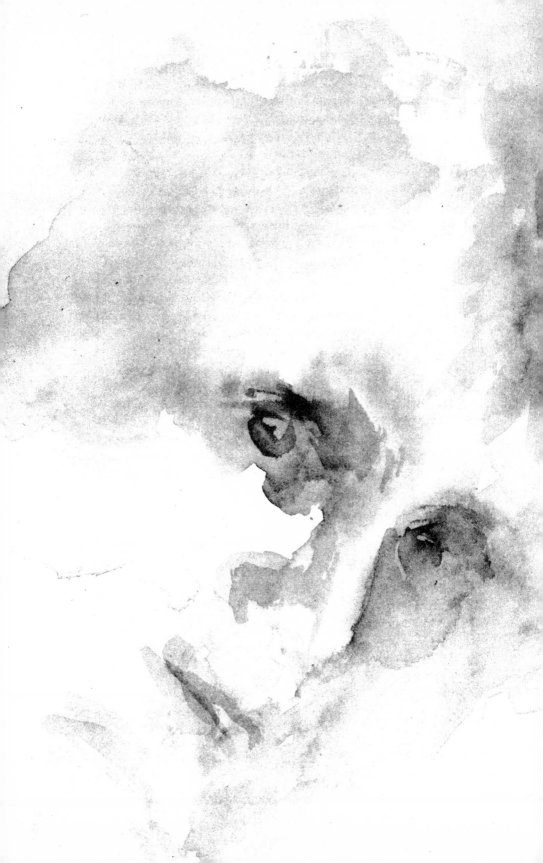

Just when the dream had first owned him, the man was not sure. He knew it had begun to overtake him before he had moved to the city. But whether the dream had been a gift from his family, or from the sea, or from his own spirit he was not sure. He only knew that this one dream now possessed him — more than did his family, or his job, or anything he owned. If it were at all possible for the dream to be fulfilled, all else would fall into place.

If one has ever been owned by a dream, then one knows the tension created. It is a two-edged sword, crying out to be shared in order that the vision may grow and bear fruit, but also imprisoned within for fear that experience will be repeated and both dreamer and dream will be rejected, never to live. And thus, the man lived with just such a tension. There were times when he would let slip hints of his dream. Yet no one, it seemed, would pick up the hint, or if they did, they would look at him with puzzled eyes, thinking they had misunderstood and afraid to betray their ignorance by inquiring further.

For the man himself there were times when the dream was strong, compelling him to initiate the process of birth into reality; and then at other times the dream seemed almost overpowered by the most mundane chatters of his urban culture. City politics, local taxes, the usual neighborhood gossip all took their toll — and the dream began to fade. Dreams die when they are not remembered, and there were many moments when life's demands brought the dream to the point of extinction. Yet somehow both the dreamer and the dream lived — which served to convince the dreamer even more of the dream's validity. The situation had to be faced. The dream had to be implemented or no one would ever know. He would never know. It was the paradox of life and of death — of knowing and of not knowing.

One evening, after having eaten with some friends, he walked home — very much in a pensive mood. He wondered about his dream. It caused him a great deal of agony for the answer was clouded and had no certainty. He only knew what he hoped could be. If he were wrong, if his suspicions were not correct — then nothing else mattered. Yet everything pointed to the fact that he was right. But he did not know for sure. All the pieces seemed to fit — but he would not know for sure until the last one was in place. And what if the last piece did not fit? What if he were wrong? What if the dream were just that — only a dream? In the last analysis there could be no certainty for dreams demand risk.

They walk with fear for they are created out of fragile possibilities, and no one can ever know for sure. For the man, one final question remained, "Which possibility bears the greater pain — to have died believing in a dream that failed or to have lived and never know?" It was this question which contained the paradox of the dream itself. For him the revelation could only come in death.

The rising sun turned the calendar page. It read *Friday*. On that day the man died. And the final piece did fit into place. His dream was resurrection.

In
Search
Of
God's
Tracks

It was early March, and the last of five days of retreat for me in the Trappist monastery of Our Lady of Gethsemani in Kentucky. I am not sure if Spring had been distracted in her scheduled arrival or if Winter was clinging with a particularly tenacious grip — but I do know that more than remnants of the latter remained and that the former had only barely begun to build her nest.

I had spent much of those five days introducing myself to the hills and valleys, the knobs and hollows of Gethsemani and of her spirit. The thermometer had only begun its seasonal climb when we arrived, and thus I was blessed to watch Winter roll back her blanket and to observe Spring delightfully poke her gurgling fingers across the land, beckoning the rest of life to come join her. Of the two — Winter was the more noticeably present, to be sure.

On this particular afternoon I experienced a tension within me for, on the one hand, I had begun the reentry process for my return into what some would call "normal" life, and yet, on the other hand, I still longed to meet the Father one more time before I had to leave. I visited the knobs and hollows one last time, criss-crossing previous journeys of my spirit as I criss-crossed the old trails of former days spent in search of the Father. I had left my own tracks in the snow, as had others before me and after. I came upon the tracks of deer and of rabbit, of Gethsemani's milk cows, and of Winter-Spring's birds. The snow land was pock-marked with tracks — of Winter and of Spring, of birds and of animals, of friends and of mine. It was then that I wondered if God left tracks as well. Like a catechism, I began to number my almost memorized answers, but also like a catechism, their faith was as shallow as the film of Spring that had been brushed over the tracks.

My catechism answered, "Of course God leaves tracks. All one has to do is to look at his creation and its beauty, at the interplay of seasons, and nature's delightful playtime." "No," came back my heart in reply, "for I have also seen his creation in its ugliness, and I have seen nature kill and destroy. Those are not God's tracks."

My catechism then answered, "Of course God leaves tracks. Look at his people — at the springtime smiles of joy, at the unre-quested gift of love, at the supporting words of hope." "No," answered my own heart again, "for I have also seen people at their worst. I have seen them hate, and live in greed and turn away in indifference. People are not God's tracks."

One last time my catechism answered, "Of course God leaves tracks. At least look at your own heart, at your own spirit. He has walked there often and worked that landscape in such a way that it no longer resembles the novice who once extended the in-vitation." "No," replied my own heart, "for I know myself too well. It is true, the landscape of my spirit has changed but it has not always been the Father's work. My own selfishness has been at work as well. I cannot look at my own spirit and say those are God's tracks."

In the end the catechism had no more answers to offer, and I yet wondered if God ever left any tracks. The next day the doors of Gethsemani closed behind me, and, unknown to me, my question somehow escaped the tiny cell which had been the scene of my quandry.

After I left Gethsemani, March continued to host the struggle between Winter and Spring, but it was only glimpses of the struggle that I was able to observe. The "normal" life to which I had returned quickly stole my lingering question. Indeed, so slyly and swiftly had I been kidnapped back into the outer demands of life, that I had not even become aware of the theft.

Gethsemani had given me many gifts — one of which was to bless each day with time taken alone in silence. Yet the gift had not been opened. When it was, when I at last stopped a day long enough to hear the Father's voice, the question returned and with it came the answer. "No, God does not leave tracks, for if he did, I would never stop a day to try and discover him, always thinking he must be around somewhere since I had seen his tracks."

I am thankful for those days in March when Winter lingered a bit, leaving enough snow for all of God's creatures to leave their tracks. And I am thankful to the Father who does not leave tracks.

And
Other
Such
Friendly
Dragons

Crisstt

Among the people who lived on either side of Christmas
and in the land that surrounded that very special time of love,
there lived a dragon
who in many ways was quite different than all other dragons.
The people of that land knew him as the Christmas dragon,

though many simply called him Crisstt.
It was odd indeed
that he should have been called the Christmas dragon
for, you see, Christmas was the one time of year
when he was not among the people of that land.
Crisstt was different from other dragons
in that other dragons spent most of their time in hiding.
On occasion they would come out
to scorch the land with their fiery breath
or level the hillside with the wag of their tail
or scare the people with their mighty roar.
But Crisstt, the Christmas dragon, was quite the opposite.
He was always among the people,
helping,
protecting.
Only on one occasion,
as I have said,
was he not there.
And that one time was the time of Christmas.
Early in the Christmas month,
Crisstt would disappear.
And he would be gone until early the next month.
Where he went
and what he would do
no one knew.
It was only recently that his story was discovered.
And thus what follows is the story of his secret
and the story of why the days of Christmas have no dragons.
Crisstt had not always been a friendly dragon.
In those first dragon years of his life
he was like all other dragons.
He ruled by breathing forth fiery hate.
He controlled with ferocious selfishness.
He wanted nothing more than to govern everything
with his dragon power.
And he was about to succeed
until the day came when he stood face to face
with Jonn,
a young unknown dragon slayer
who had grown up among the people who lived
in that special land on either side of Christmas.

There they stood,
alone,
Jonn
standing in the shadow of the fiercest dragon of the land
and already feeling the heat of Crisstt's fiery breath
even before it shot forth,
and Crisstt,
looking at Jonn
whose youth made him seem to be more a boy
than a man who slew dragons.

Then Crisstt noticed that Jonn wore no armor,
carried no shield,
wielded no sword.
It confused Crisstt.
And in that brief moment of confusion,
Jonn rushed forward,
scampered beneath Crisstt's mighty chest
and grabbed on to the end of Crisstt's powerful tail,
for, you see, the end of a dragon's tail
is the one, weak, vulnerable spot of a dragon's body.
With a jerk and a twist,
swifter than the blink of a dragon eye,
Crisstt was on his side,
overpowered by the youthful wisdom of his foe.
He waited to be slain by the blade of his own sword
now held in Jonn's hand,
but instead Jonn simply smiled a wish of peace.
"No, my dragon friend," he said,
"I shall not slay you,
for it is the night of Christmas.
It is the one night of peaceful love — even for dragons."
And with that Jonn let go of the powerful tail,
laid down the sword,
turned
and walked away.
So moved by such an act of kindness,
so dumbfounded by those few words,
so amazed by the fearlessness of such youth,
Crisstt simply sat there,
now totally changed by the love that had been shown him.
It was then
at that very moment
that Crisstt decided he would no longer be the dragon he once was.
From that Christmas hence,
Crisstt always spoke love instead of breathing fiery hate.
Rather than destroy fields,
he used the power of his tail to help the people plow fields.
He turned his ferocious selfishness
into ferocious kindness.
From that Christmas on,
Crisstt was a dragon like no other dragon.

But there is more to the story,
for there is yet to be explained the secret
of Crisstt's yearly disappearance during the time of Christmas
as well as the reason why even today
the days of Christmas have no dragons.
It all came about in the following fashion.

Impressed by the kindness shown him
and by the love he had discovered,
Crisstt then decided
that more than anything else
he wanted to repay Jonn
and the people who lived on either side of Christmas.
And so he went about his task.

Being a dragon himself
and knowing well dragon ways,
Crisstt knew that within each person there lived a dragon —
quiet, small, yet nevertheless a dragon
who came out in many ways.
There were grey dragons of hate
who caused people to be unkind.
There were purple dragons of selfishness
who would not let people share.
There were green dragons of greed
and red dragons of hurt.
Crisstt knew that in everyone there was a dragon,
and sometimes people gave in to their dragons
and let them rule.
But Crisstt also knew that the time of Christmas
was the one time of the year
when people should be free from their dragons.

And so it was that in the weeks before each Christmas,
while everyone slept,
Crisstt would go from heart to heart,
from spirit to spirit,
and he would invite the dragon that lived in each
to a special banquet that would last for days woven into weeks.
By the time the day of Christmas arrived,
Crisstt would have touched every heart in the land,
and every dragon would have been invited to the banquet.

There at the banquet Crisstt made provisions
for all the best in dragon food and drink.
There was music and laughing and the telling of dragon stories.
It became the one event of the entire dragon year
that no dragon would ever miss.
It was so attractive to all the dragons
that by the time they would get bored
and want to go back to the hearts and spirits
from which they had come,
it would always be well past Christmas.
Why, you ask, did Crisstt do this?
The answer is simple —
so that during the days of Christmas
there would be no dragons,
no dragons of hate or selfishness,
none of greed
or power
or hurt.
And now you too know the secret of Crisstt,
the Christmas dragon,
and why during the days of Christmas
he would disappear from among Jonn
and the people who lived on either side of Christmas.
And so it is that each year
during the days of Christmas
people again learn to live in peace.
They gift one another with understanding,
and selfishness seems to become a once-upon-a-time way of life.
Evil is conquered by goodness,
and hate is overcome with kindness.
Generosity rules over greed,
and the only power that reigns is the power of love.
For, you see, it is true —
the days of Christmas have no dragons.

I
Would
Rather
Be
Bread

(The following is a dialogue meditation intended to be read aloud by two individuals. It is meant to be interpreted freely and creatively.)

Reader 1
If you had your choice,
which would you rather be?

Reader 2

Huh? What would I rather be?

Uh huh.
Would you rather be bread,
or would you rather be a stone?

Oh. I guess I'd rather be bread.

Bread?

Uh, huh.

I'd rather be a stone.
You can't build a house
out of bread.

You can't build a family
out of stones.

Stones are strong.

But bread, when it's shared
is even stronger. Did you
ever share a stone?

What good is the bread
once it's shared? It's gone.
And what have you got left?
But with a stone...

what you've got left is...
a stone.

At least you've got something.

I think I'd rather be bread.

If I asked you for a stone,
would you give me bread?

If I asked you for bread,
would you give me a stone?

You're not fair.

Hungry people would
rather have bread.

But I'm not hungry.

So you'd rather be a stone.

I wouldn't want to be bread.

Hungry people would love you.

And then I'd be all used up.

But they wouldn't be hungry.

And I wouldn't be! Period!

But you are now?

I am now what?

You're *being*???

I'd rather be a stone.

I'd rather be bread.

If I asked you for a stone,
would you give me bread?

If I asked you for bread,
would you give me a stone?

Stones are good for sitting on.

Bread is good for sitting with.

Stones are good for throwing.

Bread is good for giving.

Stones are always the same —
strong and solid. You can
be secure like a rock.

Or cold like a stone.

Or stale like yesterday's bread.

Or useless like one
in a million stones.
I'd rather be bread.

I'd rather be a stone.
Stones are good for
making slippery ways rough,

and smooth lives bumpy.
But bread can make a
bumpy life smooth.

If you like breaded life.

Rather than stoney living.
Stones don't care.

And bread does?

When it's shared.

If I asked you for a stone,
would you give me bread?

If I asked you for bread,
would you give me a stone?...

When
All
The
Other
Angels
Had
Failed

Having completed his creation, God looked at all that he had made and saw that it was good. But it was his creation of man and woman that gave him the most delight for they were made in his image — in the image of love. And so it was that he wanted them, most of all, to know that he would always be with them.

He called representatives of all of his creation together. Delegations from rock and from fire, from sky and from earth were present. Grass and trees as well sent their delegates. And every kind of animal — wild and tame, crawling and swimming, walking and flying — was notified of its right to attend the assembly.

God ushered them into his largest vaulted assembly hall, and he made known to them his intention to give to his people a sign of his love, a sign of his continued presence among them. The question he placed before the rest of his creation was "Who should I send?"

The heavens almost collapsed as the thundering cries arose. "Send me!" "Send me!" "No, no, send me!" It was indeed a dilemma for God, for all of his creation wished to be the one sent as a sign of his love and presence. He was pleased, yet what was he to do?

In the midst of all of the noise, it was water in the front row that drew God's attention. For while all of the others made much noise, water was able to splash and spray and in this way take hold of God's notice. And so God motioned to his angels to sound the trumpet and call for silence. Once all had settled down, God said to water, "Tell me, water, why it is that you think you should be chosen as the sign of my love and my presence among the people I have created."

"It is because I am so necessary for life," said water. "Whenever your people see me, they will think of the life I bring, and they will remember the life you have given them, and they will know that you love them and are with them."

"Very good," said God. "I have created well, for my creatures know my ways. Water, I hereby send you to my people. May they know that I love them and am with them." And with that, water went down among the people.

In the beginning all went well. Where the people found water, there they also remembered that God loved them and was with them. But soon his people grew accustomed to the presence of water and began to forget its message. With this, water found it difficult to cope. His fear of losing his position as God's messenger drove him to desperation. He became more and more angry — so angry that he began to flood God's earth and God's people. And then it was that he became not the sign of life but the sign of death. And thus it was that God was forced to call back his sign of love and presence, for water had failed.

Shortly thereafter, wind blew up to God and said, "Send me, God, as the sign of your love and your presence among your people. I will do much better than water."

"Tell me," said God, "why you think you can do so much better than water?"

Here was the opportunity wind had hoped for. "You see, O God," began wind, "I will be able to slip up to your people quietly in a gentle breeze and cool them in the heat of the day. And should they ever begin to forget — as they did with water — I will be able to blow strong and loud so that I cannot be missed. And in addition, I will be able to dry up the flood which water left behind. Send me, God, for I will do well."

"Very good," said God. "I have created well, for my creatures do know my ways. Wind, I hereby send you to my people. May they know that I love them and am with them." And with that wind went down among the people.

Like water, the beginning proved successful for wind. He cooled them with a gentle breeze and the people remembered God's love and his presence. And when they would begin to forget and take wind for granted, he would howl and swirl, and the people would take notice. But in time, the people even became accustomed to wind's strength. The problem was that while they could hear wind, they could not see him and the people slowly began to forget and be indifferent. And thus it was that God was forced to call back his sign of love and presence, for, like water, wind too had failed.

God was about to resign himself to the fact that none of his creation would be able to speak well enough of his love and presence to his people, when cloud slipped in under the door. "Yes," said God. "What can I do for you? Not more problems, I hope."

"On the contrary," said cloud. "I am the solution to your problem of sending someone among your people."

"You? Why you?" asked God. "Why should you be any better than water or wind?"

"Because I am the best of both," said cloud. "I am made of a dewy mist so that I might give life just as water, and I bring with me a gentle wind to drift and to cool. Yet, unlike wind, I can be seen. With me your people will know that you love them and are with them."

"Very good," said God. "I have created well, and my creatures truly do know my ways. Cloud, I hereby send you to my people. May they know that I love them and am with them." And with that, cloud went down among the people.

Cloud was successful, just as she had promised. She brought life-giving water and refreshing breezes. And God's people once again knew of God's love and his ever continuing presence. And because cloud could be seen by the people, they did not forget — at least not too often — for cloud's only problem was that as soon as hot sun came, cloud disappeared. Try as she might, she could not last through the day. And thus it was that God was forced to call back his sign of love and presence, for, like water and like wind, cloud too had failed.

And so it was that for eons and eons, God's people did not know of his love and his presence. In no way was God able to discover a means of making himself known to his people. And those made in the image of love lived out their existence unaware of the presence of that love. It was a lonely time, indeed, both for God and for his people.

Then one day, in the quiet of his creation, bread came to God and said, "Your people are crying out in hunger, O God. They cry out that you have forgotten them for they have no food. Send me as a sign that you love them and are with them. They will not be able to forget me for they will be in need of me every day. They will not be alone when they discover that you are with them for I beg to be shared, and so I will call them together. When they come together to share in me, your bread, then they will know that you love them and are with them. I am the sign for which you have searched so long."

It seemed too good to be true, thought God. Had he really discovered the sign of his love and his presence. Perhaps it was worth the risk. He would send bread.

Bread came among his people. They shared that gift of bread and they shared in their Father's love. And that is why from that day until this day, when people come together to share bread, they know that God loves them and is with them.

From
Sea
To
Shining
Sea

The constant, shoreline skirmish between land and sea is the only remaining testament to the battle once waged in cosmic fury between those same two forces. Now all that remains is the simple quiet give-and-take between wave and beach played out for our benefit. And when there is danger that our memories may lose hold of the power which once belonged to them both, it is the sea who unleashes her waves of foaming thunder upon the land, and the land who catapults his cliffs into the sea hoping that her power might be crushed. Yet, for the most part all that remains is the quiet skirmish along the shore.

It began — and it ended — during the time of Genesis. Both Sun and Moon had already been shotput into existence, and Wind had been breathed forth both as whispered breeze and clamoring storm. And then there was also Land, and there was Sea. Limits had not yet been set — nor as yet determined to be necessary. Consequently, Sun and Moon jealously maneuvered for control of the heavens — totally unaware of what went on beneath. Wind, not yet forced into coexistence with Rain and Cloud and Snow, ruled with delightful abandon. Finally, Land and Sea fought for control of the earth. For the most part, that is how it began and how it ended. That is how it still continues.

Both Land and Sea sensed the question, "Who was to rule earth?" Both wished to author the answer in their own script. As much as anyone can tell, it seemed that initially both had been allotted relatively equal space. And, since owned space is one determinant of power, each jealously preserved their space.

Land signed his space with jagged mountain peaks — domineering, impressive, controlling. There was no way Sea could overcome the imposing power they signaled. Without doubt, it had seemed, Land had taken the initiative. Land had climbed higher, had acquired more space in the process, was more visible, and now seemed in control. Yes, Land had become number one, and he felt quite content with himself.

How foolish, however, for Land to believe that Sea would allow herself to be outranked so quickly and so easily. While Land had climbed high, Sea had grown calm and reflectively placid, lying in still anticipation beneath Land's symbols of power, lying beneath the orchard tree waiting for the ripened fruit to drop into her basket. And when Land had completed his task, feeling quite content, he gazed down upon Sea and saw his own reflection. His jagged peaks shook, almost trembling. What good was being number one, if he could be so easily duplicated. Land and mirrored land, peak and mirrored peak — who could know the difference? who would care? who would be impressed? who is there to rule and control if all are equal?

Thus it was that Sea now seemed to be number one — for she was all that Land was. She reflected perfectly his height, his space, his visibility. And in addition, she could overcome by the force of her moving waters; she could refresh by her coolness; and in time she would rain life on the yet unformed green growth.

Though impressed with herself, Sea lusted for more. It was not enough to be number one. If there were space yet capable of being possessed, she desired it. If she could be more visible, she sought after it. If she were able to gain more control, she craved it. She sought to control by being the sole force for existence.

Slowly, almost imperceptibly, Sea began to wash Land's shore. Without notice she washed Land away, weathering the rock, eroding the sand, undermining the cliffs — and Land was loosing. But Land fought back. He would send a peak crashing into Sea, pushing her back beyond where she had begun. In her quest for more space Sea would fill the valleys, but Land would lift one end of the valley, emptying her back into the basin. In her search for more power Sea would batter away at Land's rocky cliffs, yet Land would build breakwaters and shape coves, restraining Sea's effectiveness. All that mattered was the more of what already Sea possessed. Without more, Sea could not understand how she could be happy. Thus the passionate quest by Land and Sea continued for unknown stretches of eternity. For the most part, as I said, that is how it began and how it still continues. Yet there is a mystic ending, webbed in between.

There came a time when Sea outlasted Land in their passionate quest for more. Land was broken down and humiliated. No longer could he even feign superiority, for his jagged peaks, once symbols of control, had been reduced to smooth bald skulls — kindly left as tokens of past glory to a dying old man, senile and helpless. In the end, Sea's passion for more had prevailed. Yet in that victory was her defeat. As she conquered — she was divided. Where she was once deep and clear, she became shallow and muddied. She could no longer reflect the beauty and the majesty about her — in part because she had destroyed it and there was none to reflect, and in part because she had destroyed her own ability to reflect.

As she acquired more, she also acquired death. Because of her vast surface and shallow depth she began to be evaporated by Sun and its heat, who had long before found the wisdom to create peace with Moon. Lacking in her previous beauty and therefore ignored by Wind, Sea began to become stagnant and sick. She died in her search for more. Both Land and Sea had been reduced to powerlessness by the attainment of power, and to non-existence by the spacial acquisition of existence.

Yes, that is how it ended — and how it began — and, for the most part, how it still continues. Walk along the shore and watch the quiet skirmish between wave and beach — between Sea and Land. It is the ever-continuing quest for more — from sea to shining sea.

It is the American Dream.

Of
Truths
And
Untruths

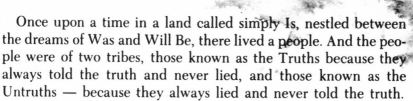

Once upon a time in a land called simply Is, nestled between the dreams of Was and Will Be, there lived a people. And the people were of two tribes, those known as the Truths because they always told the truth and never lied, and those known as the Untruths — because they always lied and never told the truth.

In the beginning all went well. Everyone knew to which tribe they belonged and to which tribe everyone else belonged. And life was simple — they only made friends with those in their own tribe.

As time passed and many generations had lived in the land, people did not always remember who belonged to which tribe. In time they became more and more conscious of the problem — who belonged to which tribe? For, you see, if you asked a Truth to which tribe he belonged, he would answer, "To the Truths," because he always told the truth. And if you asked the same question of an Untruth, he also would answer, "To the Truths," because he always lied and never told the truth. And thus it was that it did become rather confusing.

As time went on, Truths and Untruths began to marry one another simply because no one knew who was who. And the children they bore had within them a bit of truth and a bit of untruth. Eventually everyone was a mixture of both even though all thought and insisted that they were pure truth. Yet in reality, everyone who lived in the land of Is had within them that which was of Truth and that which was of Untruth.

One day a stranger came into their land — a stranger who was pure Truth, though no one recognized him. He always spoke the truth and never lied. And so it was that when he saw the truth in someone, he would tell that person of the goodness he saw. But just as honestly, whenever he saw the untruth in them, because he always told the truth, he would tell them of that which was not so good as well. Yet he did this, not because he wished to hurt them, but because he loved them. It was his hope, you see, that when someone could see what about them was true and what about them was untrue, they would know what to keep and what to root out. In that way, he hoped they would gradually become more and more true.

The people of Is, when hearing of the truth in them, would be very happy and delighted. However, when it was the untruth within which they had to see, they became very angry indeed. And thus it was that the stranger, who was truth and who had come to heal, in the end caused division and pain precisely because he was truth. And in the end, the people of Is, unable to face their own untruth, gathered together and killed the stranger who was truth.

And The Three Trees Died

Against the dense semi-wilderness of Davenport Bay stood three trees denuded of life. Tombstones to death, they cried louder in their silent graves than did the lush life surrounding them. Why, one wondered, were those three chosen for death in the midst of so much life? Had they squandered life or been choked by hoarding life? Were their deaths vestiges of what once was or seeds of what would be? Whose hand had done the choosing — fate's? A human scavenger's? their own?

What follows, then, is the story of the three dead trees. Its truth lies beyond history and is sewn into the fabric of all creation. Its truth is that hue of reality which colors all that is, yet which is so fragile that if one looks too harshly, its gentle shades wash pale.

The story of the first tree began shortly after he realized that he indeed would survive, for all too often young seedlings fail to overcome the imposing self-importance of youthful winter's first cold or the power-hungry drought of middle-aged summer. He realized with a selfish delight that he alone dominated the shore line. It seemed so foolish to him to share the water's edge. Thus it was that he decided to grow straight and tall, giving forth few branches. He had come to know, from the trees in the fields behind, that branches meant buds, and buds meant seeds and new

life, and therefore few branches meant few seeds. He had decided to keep the shoreline to himself, growing sleek and tall, reaching for life unlimited without the burden of bearing fruit or sharing resources. Unknowingly he reached death, for without branches and their leaves he was unable to gather the sun. In time, the sun that could have formed him into one who reigned over the shore, instead shaped him into a grey spear of death, surrounded by the very trees which he chose not to birth.

It was shortly after the death of the first tree, yet long before the tall green wild edged the shore that the story of the second tree began. She had come to know the story of the first tree, yet she had grown blind to her own copied cunning. She too lusted for ownership of the shore line and had decided to achieve it by growing broad and gnarled, choking off all that would sprout forth beneath her, even the fruit of her own seeds. Yet in her preoccupation with dominance, she grew unaware of innocent seedlings growing taller than she. In time the seedlings became trees and, taller than she, choked off the sunlight much as she had choked off previous growth. Finally what remained was a crown of brambled branches, the vestige of a reign once claimed — a monarchy overthrown.

Finally comes the story of the rusty pine — a promise to be ever-green broken by an outward choice turned inward. As in the first two stories, this tale too begins with a decision to dominate the shore. Yet, while the first two tales tell of desires for life turned rancid in the choosing, the final tale is a choice for life through death becoming a twisted mockery of the resurrection.

Like the others, the pine too lusted for the shore, yet realized his limited power to control. It was his thinking that if the others discovered him beginning to die, they would choose not to come

to the shore for fear of their own death. Thus the pine began to die, but only from the bottom, and only a small portion. The others, however, continued to seed themselves about him, and thus the pine chose to die a bit more. The process of new growth and the pine's dying continued until one day when the pine gave forth the final touch of life. There was no more of his life which remained — all had been given over, yet all for the wrong reason. The burnt brown needles remained as a testimony of how death for the sake of life ends in death when it is chosen not for others but for oneself. It is the right thing done for the wrong reason.

Today the three dead trees yet stand in Davenport Bay. They are witnesses to the forces of death woven into life. Yet it is a blessing and not a curse for we have been given a choice between life and death. And if we ever look into the soul of our choices and find our spirits rigid and grey, or brambled with selfishness, or colored in rust, then we will know that we have chosen death. Yet we must also know that, unlike the three dead trees, we make our choices anew each morning, and tomorrow need not be like yesterday for we have been blessed, not cursed, with today.

Once
Barefoot
And
Thirsty

Alone, deep in thought, God searched for the way by which he could be among his people. They were not yet ready, he thought, for him to make himself completely and totally known to them. He needed a sign, an action, some way of helping them understand that he was indeed with them. And then it came — with a flash of heavenly light that startled even his closest advisors. Sharing. That's what it would be. If his people could be taught to share, then they would know that he shared his love with them and that he was with them. But what was it that they were to share?

God looked down among his people and he saw many of them often cold and with little to wear. And so he made known to them through their leaders that they should share their shoes with one another.

And the people did as they were told — they shared their shoes. Yet they did not know that God was with them.

The problem that seemed to come up immediately was that now there was a nation of people — all of whom had only one shoe. And so people were either hopping around on one foot, or limping because one foot was higher than the other. Eventually, almost all of them set aside their one shoe and simply went barefoot — and still very cold.

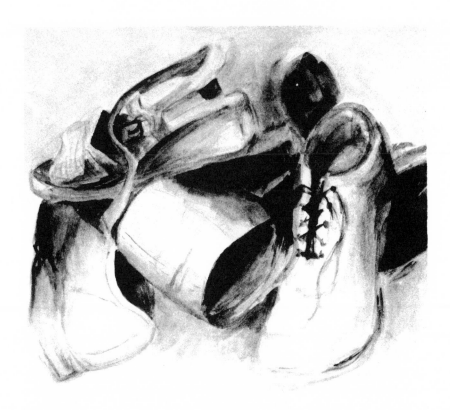

In his desire to be with his people, God once again looked down among them, and, because they lived in the desert, he saw many of them thirsty. And so he made known to them through their leaders that they should share their water with one another.

And the people did as they were told — they shared their water. Yet they did not know that God was with them.

The problem seemed to be that they had few cups or bowls. And so they would cup the water in their hands to carry it to their neighbor. But the water, as water always does, quickly ran out between their fingers. And as it turned out, no one had water — not those who carried it, nor those who were to receive it. And God's people were still thirsty with nothing to share so that they could know that he was with them.

God looked down upon his people once again. There they were, his people, and they did not even know that he loved them. There was nothing they could share. Except!!! That was it!!! Of course!!! They could share bread. They could share bread and still have plenty for themselves — not like the shoes. They could share bread and not loose it — as happened with the water. They could share bread and be together when they did. They could be happy and not hungry. They could be strength for one another. And so God made known to them through their leaders that they should share their bread with one another.

And the people did as they were told — they shared their bread. And from that day on they knew that God was with them.

The Bottle

My steps traced the dancing shoreline of the lake as I allowed my mind to wander through the misty waves of sea spray. Something within me sensed the strangeness of that day as I came upon a bottle delivered by the waves to the waiting shore. I picked up the bottle and held it against the sun, hoping to see the treasure of a message set down by unknown hands. But the bottle was empty — there would be no story to tell, no future for me to enter.

I took notice then that the bottle had a cork. Whether its purpose was to seal in or to seal out, I was not sure, yet for some reason the cork seemed most unusual. Slowly I pulled the cork from the bottle, and then... the bottle began to sing...

I will tell you of my story and the Spirit drunk from me.

I will tell you of my story and the gifts which are now free.

Startled, I put the cork back into the bottle and stood there, not knowing or understanding.

Not far from where I stood, wedged into the sand, there was a large log which the waves had washed upon the shore. I walked over to the log and sat down. I looked at the bottle — wondering what to do. For the second time, I carefully pulled the cork out of the bottle, and again the bottle sang...

I will tell you of my story and the Spirit drunk from me.

I will tell you of my story and the gifts which are now free.

And so I took the bottle and gently placed it in front of me upon the sand. I sat there, upon that log, and listened to the bottle and its story.

A long, long time ago, when the moon rose in the morning and the sun rose at night, when all of creation was still turned downside up and outside in, there was a tiny village tucked between the sun and the moon, between darkness and light, yesterday and tomorrow. In that village there lived many people. There were cobblers and blacksmiths, and bakers and barbers, and shepherds and doctors, and teachers and farmers. They all lived in that village, and all had talents and gifts. But alas, the people with the gifts were beginning to die, and thus the gifts themselves were dying as well. Yet no one knew why.

The doctor, who had the gift to heal, was himself sick. And the teacher, who had the talent to bring learning to others, was herself not learning. The farmer, who had fields ready for the harvest, grew poor as he watched his crops spoil for no one came to buy his food and share in his goodness. And thus it was that the village which was home to all kinds of people, to cobblers and blacksmiths, and bakers, and barbers, and shepherds and doctors, and teachers and farmers, — that village which had so many gifts was now dying.

One night, when the sky was at its darkest and when the clouds were so black that one could not even see one's own darkness, much less one's neighbor's darkness, when everyone had laid their weary bodies to rest, a stranger slipped unseen by anyone into the village. He immediately found his way to the well in the center of the village. There he took out from within his coat a bottle. He pulled out the cork...

Then he poured the bottle of Spirit into the well and slipped out away from the village.

When morning came, the villagers made their usual walk to the well for their daily supply of water. All the villagers came to the well — the cobblers and the blacksmiths, and the bakers and the barbers, and the shepherds and the doctors, and the teachers and the farmers. They all drank, that day, of the water from the well. They all drank of the one Spirit.

That day marvelous things began to happen in the village. The doctor decided that even though he himself was not well, he would go about and bring healing to all the others who were sick. As he brought the gift of healing, he began to notice the smiles on the faces of those whom he healed. Those many smiles made him feel so good that soon he himself began to feel much better. Soon the doctor found himself being healed as well.

The teacher who had stopped learning decided that she would go out among the people and share what knowledge she had with whoever would listen. As the people of the village learned, they began to come back to her to learn more. And soon the teacher needed to study more so that she would have more to share. Thus she learned more as well.

The farmer? He looked at his fields ripe for harvest and decided that he would at least give away the food before it began to spoil. So he went from door to door sharing his food. And the people who were strengthened by his food began to return to the farmer to buy more. Thus he grew more food, and he himself had more food and found that he and his family became more and more healthy.

On that marvelous day the same happenings were repeated among all the people of the village, for all who had gifts began to share their gifts. It was the day when the cobblers and the blacksmiths, and the bakers and the barbers, and the shepherds and the doctors, and the teachers and the farmers all drank of the one Spirit.

Well, I sat there on the log, gazing at the bottle and dreaming of, the story it had just shared. Again it sang...

Gently I lifted the bottle from the sand and replaced the cork, now knowing that its purpose was to seal in and not to seal out. Then I walked over to the shore of the lake and, with a bit of sadness, returned the bottle and its story to the sea from whence it had first come. The waves then came and carried their story back out to the depths of that silent sea.

The
Silly
Easterlies
Of
Halloween

Each year as October departs she dresses her children in fantasies and dreams borrowed from other worlds. Ghosts and goblins battle witches and monsters for trick-or-treat doorbells. Angels walk hand-in-hand with devils, and cowboys join Indians in nighttime raids for candied booty. It is October's season of Halloween.

The Autumn winds have carried many tales of how the time of Halloween came about. The winds of the North tell of our need to dress as ghosts and goblins and witches in order to hide ourselves from the real spirits of darkness, who on one night a year come in search of humans to add to their numbers. The windy gusts of the West insist that we dress in ghoulish disguises in order to frighten the evil spirits into thinking that we are more evil than they. The breezes of the South teach us to dress as holy people, as saints or as angels, hoping the spirits of darkness will think it of no use to tempt us. And the easterlies? — they have always been thought to be silly winds, spinning and tumbling, never serious enough to know or discover what is real and true. Yet this is their tale and, while you yourself must weigh its merit, I can only say that too often those who are thought to be least wise speak with a wisdom most profound.

It was a cool and cloudy Autumn afternoon when I overheard the tale told by the last easterlies of the season. Though Winter's winds had already begun to gather in the North, the few remaining easterlies lingered behind a small ruffle of a hill to play among some young oaks. They were preparing the oaks, as I later came to know, for the wisdom they would one day be expected to possess. The story they shared is the story I now share with you.

A long, long time ago, in the days when people were yet selfish and before they had learned to share their love and live in peace with one another, the season of Autumn was in constant battle with the people of Autumn. The season, it seemed, bore fruit for all of creation. Indeed, it was a harvest of great abundance for all of God's creatures — grain for the deer and the cattle and corn for the birds, fallen apples for raccoons and for foxes, nuts for the squirrels, and honey for the bears and carrots for the rabbits. Yet the greatest delight was that there was enough of each of the harvest fruits for all of the people of Autumn to share with one another. No one — neither people nor animals — lived in need.

Nevertheless, because in those days the people had not yet learned how to share, the people of Autumn began to gather and to hoard. They were not content to simply have enough to meet their day to day needs. For a time, the season of Autumn was able to satisfy the people's selfishness and keep up with their demands. Yet before long, the wants of the people became greater than the season's ability to provide. As a result, all of God's other creatures began to grow weak from the lack of food.

God worried about his creation and yet hesitated to interfere, for since he created out of loving freedom, it would seem quite contrary now to make demands upon his people. Love that is not free is not love anymore than God without love is God. God needed to send a gentle reminder — not a demand, or a law, but a simple hint that he was not pleased with such goings on.

It was then that he chose the easterlies as his messengers (at least according to their story). Because they were such silly winds, no one would take them overly seriously. Yet because they were

winds, they would not be ignored. And so it was that the silly easterlies related to the people of Autumn the Creator's displeasure concerning their hoarding.

Whatever the change in attitude among the people of Autumn, it was not long lasting. It seemed that their selfishness was too much a part of their lives — indeed, it had been with them almost from the beginning. In their cunning they made plans to continue their hoarding in secret. Thinking they could disguise their selfishness to seem like childlike play, they hoped to be able to fool both God and the season of Autumn into thinking they had given up all selfish hoarding.

On the last night of October all of the people gathered together and wove a plan as dark as the night. Everyone dressed in a costume — a disguise of one sort or another. There were those whose purpose was to frighten the season of Autumn into giving over her harvest. They dressed as witches and as monsters, as goblins and as ghosts and as devils. They stained the night with their selfishness as they ran through the darkness. Everytime they would bump into the season of Autumn they would scare her into filling their sacks with her harvest, with apples and nuts and sweet bread.

There were also those whose intent was to deceive God and the season of Autumn by goodness and kindness. They dressed as angels and holy people, hoping that the season of Autumn would give them her harvest for safe keeping lest it be stolen by all those

witches and goblins. And they did succeed in their deceit—at least with the season of Autumn. On the first morning of November, the morning after all the costumed trickery, the land lay barren. There were no apples on the trees; the fields were empty and without crops; gardens lay naked, stripped of their produce. All of the earth was black and white and gray. There was no color because there was no love.

God, on the other hand, had not been fooled. He had watched it all and he was saddened, for it was still a time when people were yet selfish, when they had not yet learned to share their love and live in peace with one another. While on the one hand, God did not want to punish them even though they had misused the gift of their freedom, on the other hand, God thought it necessary that they learn the ways of love and peace and sharing. As a result, God called the first day of November "All Saints Day" for it was the day after the costumed trickery, and his people needed to be reminded of what they could be if they shared with one another. They could be saints — not because of their costumes but because of their love.

Now you too know the story of the silly easterlies told to the young oaks behind the hill. You know too why October is filled with so much color and why November comes dressed in black and in gray. And you now know why October departs dressed in costumed fantasies borrowed from other worlds and why November begins with the "Day of All Saints." But most important of all, you know that once, a long, long time ago, people were yet selfish for in those days they had not yet learned to share their love and to live in peace with one another.

If
Not
For
Our
Unicorns

Just when it was that he and Chisel had first met, Toby could never quite remember. To him it seemed that they had been friends from the beginning — which is almost the way it had been. Now Toby was at that age when little boys begin growing up and when dreams of what could be mysteriously become memories of what once was. And Chisel — well Chisel had never grown older, for growing old is caused by needing love, and Chisel had always been loved by Toby.

Though Toby seemed to have forgotten and Chisel only faintly remembered, the two had first met in a Christmas dream. It had begun as a lonely dream, and Toby had found himself lost in the middle of a large, dark forest where the wind cried instead of whistled and where leaves turned grey instead of orange and gold. There was no light and no friends and Toby was all alone. Frightened and confused, Toby sat down beneath a tree and squeezed his eyes tight so that none of his light could slip out into the dark forest. Then, in the quiet, he heard a voice whisper:

Forest shadows and black moonbeams
Sprinkled with love turn to Christmas dreams.

Toby wondered whether or not he should open his eyes. Perhaps it was the forest trickster eager to snatch away his light, or, on the other hand, it could be a forest wizard willing to share new light. Toby wasn't sure and he hesitated, knowing that when his eyes were squeezed tight his light could not escape, yet also knowing that new light could not slip in.

Then he heard it again:

Forest shadows and black moonbeams
Sprinkled with love turn to Christmas dreams.

Finally curiosity conquered and pried open Toby's eyes. What he saw first startled him, but then, as little boys will, Toby began to smile and giggle. There, in front of him, stood a unicorn — shy and bashful. The unicorn asked Toby why he was laughing, and Toby simply explained, "You look so silly — a unicorn without a horn. How come you don't have a horn like other unicorns?"

"I'm not sure," answered the unicorn. "Some say I keep loosing them. Others say I'm not old enough. And some say I need to be wiser. I really don't know." So gentle was the unicorn's voice that Toby just barely could hear and understand. Then the unicorn looked at Toby, looked down at the snow, and in a whisper said, "I'll be your friend if you promise not to laugh at me." Toby promised then, partly because he was lonely and wanted a friend, but more because the unicorn seemed so gentle and kind.

That is how it was when Toby and Chisel met. And in the days that followed they celebrated their friendship with fun and good times and Christmas light.

There were many in the village who would not believe that Chisel was real simply because they had never heard of a unicorn without a horn. Others spoke of Chisel and Toby's imaginary friend and simply smiled when anyone tried to explain. Some thought Chisel was not real because, they insisted, there was no one to see or touch. Yet those were the people who had never learned that what is real is seen with the heart and touched with the spirit. Yet others, like Toby's mother and father, believed in Chisel because they believed in Christmas and light.

As the seasons of the land began to unfold and unravel, a friendship of warmth was woven between Toby and Chisel. Toby was no longer lonely, and Chisel proudly began growing a unicorn horn — straight and shiny and filled with light. Together they spent their time exploring new hills and searching valleys in need of light. Chisel, who knew the forest ways, would lead Toby along its paths; and Toby, who was skilled in being a boy, taught Chisel the ways of living with grown ups. They laughed and sang; they discovered and learned; they grew wiser though not by growing older. And whenever Toby would get lonely, he would simply close his eyes, imagine the forest of his first Christmas dream, and whisper to the wind:

> Forest shadows and black moonbeams
> Sprinkled with love turn to Christmas dreams.

Then in a toss of light, Chisel would stand before him, filled with light and hope and joy. They were good days for Toby and Chisel, his Christmas unicorn.

One day, after Chisel and Toby had laughed and chased and played, they rested by a tree not far from the dream where they had first met long, long ago. After much light-filled silence, Chisel nudged Toby and in his own unicorn way asked, "Toby, do you remember how we first met — in a lonely dream that was turned into Christmas? Do you remember, Toby?"

Toby nodded — almost — for he remembered only a corner of that dream. So much had faded in the light of the days that had followed. "Why do you ask?" Toby wondered.

"Well," said Chisel, "I have something very special to ask of you. It won't be easy. In fact it will be very, very difficult."

"What is it, Chisel?" Toby wondered if he really wanted to know.

"There is a little girl who lives just over the hill from here. In her dreams she often comes to this forest. Her name is Molly, and when she comes, she comes as you first came — frightened, filled with darkness, very lonely. There is no Christmas in her, Toby. She needs to be sprinkled with love. I was wondering... well... maybe if..."

Toby jumped up quickly, thinking he understood, and readily agreed. "Sure, let's go help her. I'm ready."

"No, no! That's not how it can be done," sighed Chisel. "She comes in her dreams just as you first came in yours. If she is to be filled with Christmas, it must be in her dreams. There's no other way."

By now Toby was confused and unsure what Chisel was asking. He didn't understand, and yet he was afraid that perhaps he understood only too clearly.

Chisel continued. "If I bring some Christmas light into her dreams, Toby, I must leave your dreams, for I can only live in one dream at a time. I would still be with you. I would still be real, but it would be in your memories — no longer in your dreams. Yet you've been touched by Christmas, Toby. You would be strong. You have the light, and you can give it to others."

The news that Chisel, his Christmas unicorn, might soon be leaving filled Toby's eyes with tears. "There's no other way?" he asked.

"There's no other way," answered Chisel. "But it's up to you, Toby, for if dreams aren't shared they become hollow wishes and empty could've's. That's how it is with dreams. You must be the one who says 'yes' so that I can bring light to her as I once brought light to you."

"If there's no other way, Chisel, then you must go, for Christmas must be dreamed and light must be shared and the love you've taught me must continue to live." Toby closed his eyes, and as he did tears spilled down his cheeks. "Good-by, Chisel," he whispered. "I'll miss you."

"Good-by, Toby," came Chisel's farewell. "I'll miss you too. You've been a good friend."

When Toby lifted his head and opened his eyes, it was Christmas. The little boy who had once dreamed in darkness had grown wise and filled with light. And as he stood up to walk home, a unicorn horn carved out of light fell from his lap. Memories, he thought, could be as real as dreams. As Toby walked home through the forest the memory of his dream filled the darkness with light, and the wind could be heard to whisper:

Forest shadows and black moonbeams
Sprinkled with love turn to Christmas dreams.